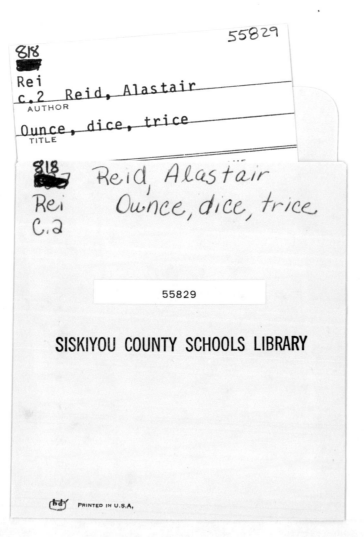

OUNCE DICE TRICE

AN ATLANTIC MONTHLY PRESS BOOK

LITTLE, BROWN & COMPANY • BOSTON • TORONTO

OUNCE DICE TRICE

BY ALASTAIR REID

DRAWINGS BY BEN SHAHN

LIBRARY OF CONGRESS CATALOG CARD NO. 58–10685

Fourth Printing

ATLANTIC–LITTLE, BROWN BOOKS
ARE PUBLISHED BY
LITTLE, BROWN AND COMPANY
IN ASSOCIATION WITH
THE ATLANTIC MONTHLY PRESS

*Published simultaneously in Canada
by Little, Brown & Company (Canada) Limited*

PRINTED IN THE UNITED STATES OF AMERICA

Introduction

This book is an odd collection of words and names, to amuse and amaze you.

Words have a sound and shape, in addition to their meanings. Sometimes the sound is the meaning. If you take a word like BALLOON and say it aloud seven or eight times, you will grow quite dizzy with it. All the words here are meant to be said aloud, over and over, for your own delight. If you want to know more about their meanings, ask a dictionary.

In the book, too, you will find some curiosities, old words no longer in use, new words which ought to exist if they do not, private family words which deserve to be better known. And if you grow to love words for their own sake, you will begin to collect words for yourself, and you will be grateful, as I am, to all the people who collect odd words and edit odd dictionaries, out of sheer astonishment and affection.

For Michael's Sake

The way to get the feel of words is to begin with a sound and let it grow. ZZZZ is the sound of someone sleeping. From it, you easily move to BUZZ and DIZZY, and soon you have a list.

ZZZZ

BUZZ

DIZZY

FIZZLE

GUZZLE

BUZZARD

BAMBOOZLE

3

Or begin with OG

and see what happens.

OG

FROG

OGLED

GOGGLE

GROGGY

TOBOGGAN

HEDGEHOG

And then you can make other lists, by
gathering together words for noises
or nightmares or things beginning
with Q. Here are some lists to guide
you.

LIGHT WORDS

(to be said in windy or singing moods)

ARIEL

WILLOW

SPINNAKER

WHIRR

LISSOM

SIBILANT

PETTICOAT

NIMBLE

NIB

HEAVY WORDS

(to be used in gloom or bad weather)

DUFFLE

BLUNDERBUSS

GALOSHES

BOWL

BEFUDDLED

MUGWUMP

PUMPKIN

CRUMB

BLOB

WORDS TO BE SAID ON THE MOVE

FLIT

FLUCTUATE

WOBBLE

WIGGLE

SHIVER

TIPTOE

PIROUETTE

TWIRL

TEETER

ODD WORDS

(to be spoken out loud, for fun)

HOBNOB

BARLEY

DOG-EARED

HOPSCOTCH

WINDWARD

OAF

EGG

OBOE

NUTMEG

OBLONG

EYE

POOP

MINIM

LEVEL

KAYAK

MARRAM

DEIFIED   REFER

WORDS THAT READ BOTH WAYS

DROWS

(read the wrong way round)

MULP

ANANAB

ROTSAC

OOBAGUB

OTAMOT

REZAGRATS

NOSAM

GUBDEB

WOLLEY

SQUISHY WORDS

(to be said when wet)

SQUIFF

SQUIDGE

SQUAMOUS

SQUINNY

SQUELCH

SQUASH

SQUEEGEE

SQUIRT

SQUAB

BUG WORDS

(to be said when grumpy)

HUMBUG

BUGBEAR

BUGABOO

BUGBANE

LADYBUG

BOGYBUG

BUGSEED

WORDS FOR TIMES OF DAY

(to be used where there are no clocks)

DAYPEEP

DAYSPRING

MERIDIAN

MAINDAY

DAYLIGONE

DIMITY

DEWFALL

GLOAMING

DUSK

OWLCRY

15

A BOOING OF BUFFALOES

A DULE OF DOVES

AN EXALTATION OF LARKS

A NYE OF PHEASANTS

A PIOLING OF PELICANS

A SKEIN OF GEESE

A SKULK OF FOXES

A SMOTHER OF SPIDERS

A SNUTTERING OF MONKEYS

A TREMBLING OF GOLDFISH

ODDS AND ENDS

A BLUNDER OF BOYS

A GIGGLE OF GIRLS

A CONSTERNATION OF MOTHERS

A GRUMBLING OF BUSES

A HUMBUGGLE OF PACKAGES

A GUNDULUM OF GARBAGE CANS

A SCRIBBITCH OF PAPERS

A TUMBLETELL OF CHURCH BELLS

A SNIGGLEMENT OF STRING

A TRIBULATION OF CHILDREN

SOUNDS

PLOO is breaking your shoelace.

MRRAAOWL

is what

cats

really say.

TRIS-TRAS

is scissors cutting paper.

KINCLUNK is a car

going over a manhole cover.

CROOMB is what pigeons

murmur to themselves.

PHLOOPH is sitting

suddenly on a cushion.

NYO-NYO is speaking with your mouth full.

HARROWOLLOWORRAH is yawning.

PALOOP is the tap dripping in the bath.

RAM TAM GEE PICKAGEE

is

feeling good.

It is most important to be a good namer, since it falls to all of us at some time or other to name anything from a canary to a castle, and since names generally have to last a long time. Here are some possible names for possible things, to give you ideas.

NAMES FOR ELEPHANTS

WILBUR ORMOND

BENDIGO BRUCE

McGRAW ROBERTSON

WENDELL TUBB DUFF

DEUTERONOMY

NAMES FOR CATS

SYBIL

CHESTER

LISSADEL

GRICE

MILDRED

FELICITY

ASTRID

JAMES BUDGE

TWEE

SINBAD

NAMES FOR INSECTS

1. TWILLITER	4. LIMLET	7. THRIMM
2. FLURR	5. TILLTIN	8. LEGLIDDY
3. TRISTRAM	6. SUMMERSBY	9. UGWOB

NAMES FOR WHALES

HUGH   BLODGE   BARNABY   HAMISH

CHUMLEY   MURDO   CHAM   OKUM   SUMP

NAMES FOR HOUSES AND PLACES

HUGG HOUSE

THE BOBBINS

BROADMEADOWS

DEERSDEN

WINDYGATES

SMITHEREENS

HOPESHAWS

OLD HULLABALOO

SMIDGIN'S NOB

DRUMJARGON

LONG STILT LANE

THE SHIVERS

FROM THE ATLAS

PEE DEE

PARSNIP

TWEED

TOMBIGBEE

OUSE

SHOSHONE

CHINDWIN

CAM

OKEFINOKEE

APP

AAR

URR

RUDE NAMES FOR NITWITS

RAPSCALLION

FLIBBERTIGIBBET

FUSSBUDGET

COYSTRIL

TAYSTRIL

JOSKIN

BUMPKIN

CLOAF

CLODHOPPER

SLAMMERKIN

NAMES FOR THE FINGERS

(always starting with the thumb)

TOMMY THUMBKINS

ETTIE WILKSON

LONG LAUDER

DAVY GRAVY

and LITTLE QUEE QUEE QUEE QUEE

or

THE EARL OF ALMOND

and LITTLE DIDO BONE

SOBER JOHN

MINNIE MILTON

TIM SUNDRY

Ani's Hand

NAMES FOR TWINS

Each pair of twins,

rabbits or dogs,

children or frogs,

has to have names

that are almost the same

(to show that they're twins)

but are different too;

so here's what you do.

Find double words,

like Higgledy-Piggledy

(good names for pigs)

or Shilly and Shally

or Dilly and Dally

or Knick and Knack.

Namby and Pamby

are better for poodles;

Whing-Ding for swallows;

Misty and Moisty

and Wishy and Washy

especially for fish.

Call twin kittens

Inky and Pinky

or Helter and Skelter,

or Pell and Mell.

(It's easy to tell

they are twins if their names

have a humdrum sound.)

Crinkum and Crankum

are perfect for squirrels,

like Hanky and Panky

or Fiddle and Faddle;

but Mumbo and Jumbo

are mainly for elephants.

(Airy and Fairy

would never suit *them*.)

Willy and Nilly

will fit almost any twins.

Hubble and Bubble

or Hodge and Podge

or Roly and Poly

are mainly for fat twins.

Chitter and Chatter

or Jingle and Jangle

or Pitter and Patter,

of course, are for noisy twins.

Further than that,

there's Harum and Scarum,

or Hocus and Pocus,

or Heebie and Jeebie,

but these are peculiar,

and have to be used,

like Mixty and Maxty,

for very *odd* pairs. . . .

You see what begins

when you have to name twins.

If you get tired of counting *one*, *two*, *three*, make up your own numbers, as shepherds used to do when they had to count sheep day in, day out. You can try using these sets of words instead of numbers, when you have to count to ten.

OUNCE

DICE

TRICE

QUARTZ

QUINCE

SAGO

SERPENT

OXYGEN

NITROGEN

DENIM

INSTANT

DISTANT

TRYST

CATALYST

QUEST

SYCAMORE

SOPHOMORE

OCULIST

NOVELIST

DENTIST

ARCHERY

BUTCHERY

TREACHERY

TAPROOM

TOMB

SERMON

CINNAMON

APRON

NUNNERY

DENSITY

ACREAGE

BROKERAGE

CRIBBAGE

CARTHAGE

CAGE

SINK

SENTIMENT

OINTMENT

NUTMEG

DOOM

Here are some odd words, either forgotten or undiscovered, with which you can bamboozle almost anyone. They are arranged in Garlands which bring you always back to the beginning. Once you have been through them two or three times, you will be able to use them whenever you wish.

WHAT IS A TINGLE-AIREY?

A *tingle-airey* is a hand organ, usually played on the street by the turning of a handle, and often decorated with mother-of-pearl or *piddock* shells.

WHAT ARE PIDDOCKS?

Piddocks are little mollusks
which bore holes in rocks and wood,
or in the *breastsummers* of buildings.

WHAT IS A BREASTSUMMER?

A *breastsummer* is a great beam
supporting the weight of a wall,
and sometimes of a
gazebo above.

WHAT IS A GAZEBO?

A *gazebo* is a round balcony with
large windows looking out on
a view, often of ornamental
gardens and *cotoneasters*.

WHAT IS A COTONEASTER?

A *cotoneaster* is a kind of
flowering shrub, a favorite
of *mumruffins*.

WHAT IS A MUMRUFFIN?

A *mumruffin* is a long-tailed tit which often visits
bird tables in winter for its share of *pobbies*.

WHAT ARE POBBIES?

Pobbies are small pieces of bread *thrumbled* up with
milk and fed to birds and baby animals.

WHAT IS THRUMBLED?

Thrumbled is squashed together. Ants thrumble
round a piece of bread, and crowds
in streets thrumble round *gongoozlers*.

WHAT IS A GONGOOZLER?

A *gongoozler* is an idle person who
is always stopping in the street
and staring at a curious object
like a *tingle-airey*.

WHAT IS FRANGIPANI?

Frangipani is a small flowering tree
which grows in tropical places, and
beside which people wearing saris
and *puggrees* walk.

WHAT IS A PUGGREE?

A *puggree* is a light scarf
worn over a hat to
protect the *paxwax* from the sun.

WHAT IS THE PAXWAX?

The *paxwax* is the tendon at the back
of the neck which supports the head,
and which flushes red when
people are in a *tirrivee*.

WHAT IS A TIRRIVEE?

A *tirrivee* is a temper.
Mothers go into a tirrivee over
the *jiggery-pokery* of children.

WHAT IS JIGGERY-POKERY?

Jiggery-pokery is trickery or
mischief or hanky-panky
on the part of children, such
as pretending to be deaf or
teasing a *Tantony*.

WHAT IS A TANTONY? A *Tantony* is the smallest pig in a litter, so called after Saint Anthony, the patron saint of swineherds. Small creatures are usually given special names, like kittens or cygnets or *quicklings*.

WHAT ARE QUICKLINGS?

Quicklings are young insects which in summer dance in the air in clouds and catch the light, looking like *moonglade.*

WHAT IS MOONGLADE?

Moonglade is the track of dancing broken light left on the sea at *dimity* by the moon.

50

WHAT IS DIMITY?

Dimity, besides being a fine cotton fabric, is the time
of day when the daylight dims, the time when, in hot
countries, men and women walk in the coolth
beside the *frangipani*.

WHAT IS A HAMBURGLER?

A *hamburgler* is a hamburger
which you creep downstairs
and eat in the middle of
the night when you
wake up hungry.
Mim people never
eat hamburglers.

WHAT ARE MIM PEOPLE?

Mim people are very proper
people who always sit with
their fingertips together and
their lips pursed tight, who
always do the right thing,
and who disapprove. Mim
people have *worgs* in
their gardens.

WHAT IS A WORG?

A *worg* is a plant which never grows. There is practically always one worg in a row of plants. You can tell it by the *gnurr* on its leaves.

WHAT IS GNURR?

GNURR is the substance which collects after periods of time in the bottom of pockets or in the cuffs of trousers. Gnurr is a smaller variety of *oosse*.

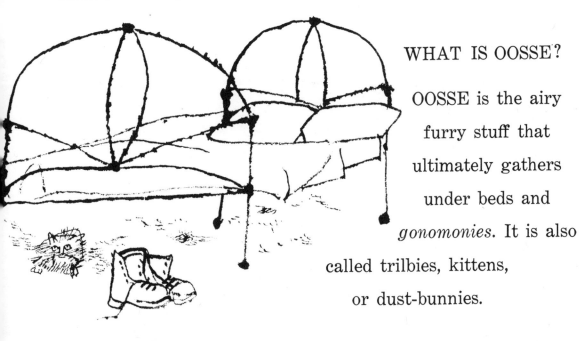

WHAT IS OOSSE?

OOSSE is the airy furry stuff that ultimately gathers under beds and *gonomonies*. It is also called trilbies, kittens, or dust-bunnies.

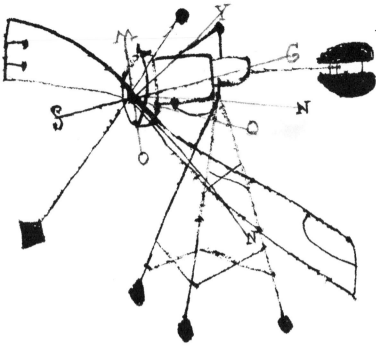

WHAT IS A GONOMONY?

A *gonomony* is any strange object that is difficult to name, that is curiously unlike anything else, and that serves no useful purpose. Gonomonies abound in the houses of *glots*.

WHAT IS A GLOT?

A *glot* is a person who cannot bear to waste anything, who stuffs his attic full of treasures which nobody else wants, and who always eats the last chocolate in the box. Glots can be recognized by the *poose* on their noses.

WHAT IS A POOSE?

A *poose* is a drop which stays
on the end of the nose and
glistens. It happens to ordinary
people when they have colds,
or when they come out of the
sea for a *chittering-bite*.

WHAT IS A CHITTERING-BITE?

A *chittering-bite* is a snack eaten after a cold
swim to keep the teeth from chattering. It may
consist of anything from an apple to a
piece of leftover *hamburgler*.

CURIOSITIES

If you want to call for silence, say

    MUMBUDGET

If you want to change
the subject, say

    PONSONBY

If you want to stop a game that
you are playing, say

BARLEY   PAX   KING'S X

KING'S RANSOM   FINS

KEYS   UNCLE

or

CRIK-CRAK

And if someone tells
you something
you don't believe,
look at him steadily
and say

FIRKYDOODLE

FUDGE

or

QUOZ